Tashi

and the
STOLEN
BUS

written by
Anna Fienberg
and
Barbara Fienberg

illustrated by
Kim Gamble

ALLEN&UNWIN

*Once, when I was in Florence, I caught a bus and
a very handsome man in a green suit got on. It wasn't
a crowded bus but the man sat down right next to me.
I was quite pleased – at first. He gave me a friendly smile
and I smiled back. Then he turned to the front and
began to bark, just like a dog. It was a loud deep bark,
and it went on all the way to the last stop, at Fiesole,
where he stood up, wagged his tail, and got off.*

*When I told Barbara about the barking man,
she laughed and said, 'I wonder what our Tashi would
do in a situation like that? What if Tashi met a stranger
on a bus–?'*

'That barked?' I said.

*In the first story Tashi does meet a stranger – a couple
of them – but he'll have to do more than wait till they get
off if he's going to save the bus...*

Have a woofing good read!

ANNA FIENBERG

Anna and Barbara Fienberg write the Tashi stories together,
making up all kinds of daredevil adventures and tricky
characters for him to face. Lucky he's such a clever Tashi.

Kim Gamble is one of Australia's favourite illustrators
for children. Together Kim and Anna have made such
wonderful books as *The Magnificent Nose and Other
Marvels*, *The Hottest Boy Who Ever Lived*, the *Tashi* series,
the *Minton* picture books, *Joseph,* and a full colour picture
book about their favourite adventurer, *There once was
a boy called Tashi.*

First published in 2006

Allen & Unwin
83 Alexander Street
Crows Nest 2065
Australia
Phone: (61 2) 8425 0100
Fax: (61 2) 9906 2218
Email: info@allenandunwin.com
Web: www.allenandunwin.com

National Library of Australia
Cataloguing-in-Publication entry:

Fienberg, Anna.

Tashi and the stolen bus.
ISBN 978 1 74114 877 0.

1. Children's stories, Australian. 2. Tashi (Ficticious character) – Juvenile
fiction. I. Fienberg, Barbara. II. Gamble, Kim. III Title. (Series: Tashi; 13).

A823.3

Typeset in Sabon by Tou-Can Design
Printed in Australia by McPherson's Printing Group

10 9 8 7 6 5 4 3

Tashi knocked on Jack's door. 'Let's catch the early bus today,' he said when Jack came out. 'We can play soccer before school.'

Jack looked down at his pyjamas. 'Okay, but instead of taking the bus let's just *walk* really fast.'

'Why?'

'I'll tell you on the way.'

When they were walking really fast to
school, Jack said, 'You know how Dad
and I caught the bus to the city
yesterday?'

'Oh yes,' panted Tashi.

'Well, this giant of a man got on at the
next stop. He stomped up the back, sat
down and then, you know what he did?
He barked like a dog!'

'Wah! What did everyone do?'

'Well, two old ladies got off quickly but
a little boy laughed and barked right back
at him.'

'Hmm,' said Tashi, as they took the
short cut through the park, 'bus trips can
be tricky. Why, I remember a bus trip back
in my village–'

Jack looked at Tashi. 'I didn't think there *were* buses in your old village.'

'Well, it was like this,' said Tashi. 'When I was very small there *weren't* any cars or buses in our village, it's true. If we had to go somewhere, we walked. So we were really excited when Teacher Pang called a meeting to tell us we might be able to start a valley bus line.'

'But how – did he win the lottery?'

Tashi grinned. 'No, Mr Pang had been talking to Can-Du, the father of a new boy at school. He told us that Can-Du was a wizard at fixing engines. He could find a broken-down rattletrap and make it go like a racing car.'

'But where would you find a bus?'

'Well, everyone knew about the old one dumped down by the river, at the edge of the forest. It had been abandoned by robbers years ago, left to the weeds and spiders. So the next day, we all pitched in to clean it out and fix the seats and fill up the holes in the floor.

'In a short time Can-Du had the engine purring, and when he put his foot down on the accelerator, it roared like a lion! We painted it a bright yellow and after a lot of argument we agreed on the name: *The Valley People's Very Own Bus Service.*

'I couldn't sleep the night before the first trip to the city. The bus was going to the markets, taking all the people who had something to sell. Grandma was making moon cakes. "You can come with me and help to sell them if you like," she said to Lotus Blossom and me.

'Well, people were already loading up cherries and apples and chickens onto the roof of the bus when we arrived.

'Can-Du had the bonnet up, checking the engine one last time. I peered in. He had already taught me about the rotor and the fan belt. I wanted to know more... But there wasn't time because, just then, two strangers moved up to talk to him. As I stepped away, I heard Can-Du arguing with them but their voices were too low for me to catch.

'The strangers didn't look like any of the villagers I knew. They wore dirty long coats and wide-brimmed hats.

'When one took his fist out of his pocket and shook it at Can-Du, I was shocked by how hairy it was. A prickle of fear flared in my chest. Wasn't there something familiar about these men? But Can-Du was standing aside now, letting them climb aboard.

'It must be all right, I thought. And wasn't this *The Valley People's Very Own Bus Service* after all? Everyone should be allowed on, hairy or not. But then, just as Grandma was about to take her seat, the two strangers pushed her aside and swaggered down the bus ahead of her.

'"No manners," muttered Not Yet, but he was careful to mutter it quietly.

'A nasty smell was coming from the men. It was like stale water in a vase when the flowers have been left to rot. Didn't I know that smell? I leant out into the aisle to get a better look and that prickly feeling in my chest exploded into panic: as one stranger swung into his seat I saw him tucking something under his coat. *A tail!*

'I looked around wildly. I tried to think what to do but the bus was packed to the brim now with people and baskets and piglets escaping, oinking up and down the aisle. And everyone was so happy, cheering and clapping each other on the back as Can-Du turned the key and the bus roared into life.

'The bus bounced beautifully along the roads and Teacher Pang shouted *"Congratulations!"* to Can-Du at the wheel. But Can-Du just hunched his shoulders and stared ahead. Maybe he knows who the mysterious strangers are, I thought. But if so, why did he let them on the bus?

'Then I noticed Mr Pang sniffing the air and wrinkling his nose. He was staring at the strangers. "I know you two!" he cried. "You're–"

'Oh Jack, his words were like a signal for everything to go wrong. Can-Du suddenly swung the wheel and veered off the road to the city, taking the track leading into the forest instead!

'"Where are you going? What are you doing?" we all shouted. Grandma's face was white and Not Yet had his face pressed against the window.

'But Can-Du seemed to have gone deaf.

'The strangers stood up and, as they did, they whipped off their hats, showing their horrible faces. "QUIET!" they bellowed. "SIT *STILL*!"

'Teacher Pang didn't obey. He leapt up and grabbed one of them by the arm. But the second stranger turned and lazily pushed him over. Teacher Pang crumpled at my feet.

'I knelt down and whispered, "You know these two, don't you?"

'"Yes, they're the demons! They raced you last year for the new school-house."

'I nodded. I could hardly breathe. "What do you think they want?"

'Before Mr Pang could answer there was a loud explosion and the bus came to a sudden stop.

'"What the *dill*blot has happened now?" The demons hurried down the bus to Can-Du.

'"I'll have to look at the engine," Can-Du answered. He opened the driver's door, but before climbing down, he beckoned to me. "I couldn't help it," he whispered. "The demons are crazy for buses! When I wouldn't hand this one over or teach them how to drive it, they kidnapped my son. They told me I would never find him again if I didn't drive the bus into the woods."

14

'"And if you want to see your boy again you will hurry up and fix this rattletrap," hissed the older demon, as he pushed Can-Du out of the bus.

'The younger demon turned to us. "This is the end of the line, you dillblots! This is where you get off because we're on our way to Xin–"

'The older demon leapt back and poked his brother hard in the back. "Hold your tongue! *You're* the dillblot, you DILLBLOT!"

'It was starting to rain and although it was still early morning the thick branches overhead and the purple sky made the forest dark and spooky.

'Grandma called out, "You can't leave us here so far from any help. We have babies amongst us and there are wolves in the forest!" Not to mention ghosts, I thought.

'The monsters shrugged; such things mattered nothing to demons. When they got out to see what Can-Du was doing, I moved over to the front window and listened hard. Soon I heard Can-Du say, "All fixed." There was just a split second to decide if I dared to do it–'

'What? What?' cried Jack.

'Well, I was in the driver's seat, wasn't I? So I turned the key in the ignition and the bus revved into a roar. Not Yct was right beside me. "Quick, Not Yet," I cried, "my feet won't reach the pedals. Can you press them down for me?"'

'Not Yet crouched down and I pointed,
"clutch down!" I put the gear into the
first position and released the brake. We
shuddered and rolled forward. I could see
the demons pulling at the door, swinging
like gorillas up the side. Grandma and
Lotus Blossom and Mrs Wang held onto
the handle with all their strength.

'"Clutch!" I cried and we moved into
second gear and went a little faster.

'"Hurry!" cried Lotus Blossom. "We
can't hold them off much longer!"

'"Clutch and accelerator together!" I sang as we jerked and bumped and rocked in a wide circle to point the bus back in the right direction. When we shot forward the demons went flying off the door like buttons bursting from a ripped seam.

'There was a stunned silence and then a great cheer went up from the passengers. They hung out the windows, jeering at the demons. "I didn't know you could drive a bus, Tashi," giggled Mrs Wang.

'"Neither did I," I said.

19

'I was sweating so much the wheel was slippery in my hands. How different it had been going for cosy little test drives with Can-Du than actually doing it myself!'

'And escaping from demons at the same time!' shivered Jack.

'Yes. You should have seen those monsters jumping up and down in the dirt, shaking their fists with rage, and hitting each other! Everyone was so busy yelling at them – and I was looking at the road ahead, of course – that we didn't notice Can-Du had flung himself on the spare tyre at the back of the bus. And now he climbed up and in through the window.

'Well, when we were at a safe distance from the demons I stopped the bus and turned around to face Can-Du. "What will we do now?"

'Everyone had an idea. But most agreed with Mr Wu. "Let's go straight to the city," he said. "I have vegetables to sell. Soon they'll spoil."

'"And my piglets won't last much longer without water."

'"And my chickens will drown up there in the rain."

'"But what about my *son?*" cried Can-Du.

'The villagers told him they would look for Little Can-Du but first they had to get to the city. So that is where we went.

'When we'd dropped most of the passengers at the markets, Grandma, Lotus Blossom, Mrs Wang, Mr Pang and I stayed behind with Can-Du to figure out how we could find his son.

'"Let's tell each other everything we know about the demons," said Mr Pang. "You start, Tashi, you're the one who has had the most to do with them."

'"We mightn't have to do all that," I said slowly. "Remember in the bus, one of the demons said that they were on their way to Xin-something? Where could that be? Is there anywhere starting with 'Xin' around these parts?"

'"What about Xinfeng?" cried Mrs Wang.

'"Of course, it's beside the mountain in the next valley," Teacher Pang agreed excitedly.

'"Which is riddled with caves – perfect places to hide something, or someone," Grandma finished up.

'We were all really pleased with each other until Lotus Blossom said, "But if it's riddled with caves, how will we find the one where Little Can-Du is hidden?"

'"Let's just get there first, and see," pleaded Can-Du, and we all agreed.

'The first creatures we saw when we reached Xinfeng were the two demons.

'"How did they get here so quickly?" I whispered.

'"They're demons," Grandma answered gloomily.

'They didn't see us because they were already busy climbing up the mountain. I cautiously followed, leaving the others waiting in the bus. There was only a thin track winding around the mountain and just as Grandma had said, the steep sides were scooped out as if a ghost monster had taken enormous bites from the rock.

'I crept along at a good distance, backing into the shadows if the demons stopped or turned around. But they hurried on, past dozens of shallow caves. Suddenly, they dived into a wide deep cave. I waited. Soon they ran out again, carrying an empty water jug. I watched in the shadows until they were out of sight and then slipped into the cave.

'It was black as night inside and I had to shut my eyes for a moment to get used to the dark. How would I find anything in this gloom?

'"Who's there?" a trembly little voice threaded through the darkness. I took a couple of steps towards the voice and made out a small bundle tied up against the wall of the cave.

'Little Can-Du cried with joy when he saw me but I told him, while I was undoing his ropes, that there wasn't any time to lose. Already demon voices were floating back. What to do?

'I spied a tall oil jar in the corner.
"Quick! Jump into this," I said, giving
him a leg-up and stuffing the ropes in on
top of him. "When the demons leave
the cave again, rock the jar till it tips
over and run down the path outside.
Your father will be waiting for
you in the bus."

'There was no time for any more. The demons were standing at the entrance of the cave. "Tashi! What are you doing here?" cried the first demon when he caught sight of me. "Where is Little Can-Du?"

'"The Grand Vizier of, er, of Zenadu took him home to his father. The Grand Vizier is very annoyed with you."

'Then I took a piece of ghost cake out of my pocket, popped it into my mouth and walked through the demons and out of the cave.

'Outside, I ducked down behind some
rocks, listening to the demons argue about
what to do. When I saw them charging
out and up the mountain, searching other
caves, I whistled softly and Little Can-Du
crept out. We tore down the hillside and
scrambled into the bus.

'"Let's go!" I cried, and so we did.

'Little Can-Du had a cuddle from Grandma and Mrs Wang while Teacher Pang and Lotus Blossom asked again and again for the story of our escape. And do you know, we were back just in time to pick up our passengers in the city.

'"Just don't expect every trip to be as exciting as this one." Can-Du smiled grimly at me, as we dropped our last passenger off.'

Jack jumped as they heard the school bell ring across the park. 'Whew! That was the strangest bus trip I ever heard of,' he panted as they began to run. 'But you know, ship cruises can be even worse.

'I mean, you can't get off a ship until you reach port, not unless you want to be eaten by sharks. My Uncle Joe had to swim for ten kilometres once, when pirates attacked his boat in the Caribbean. Imagine, he had to swim to Jamaica!'

'Now that would be a good story,' said Tashi as they hung up their bags. 'When did you say your Uncle Joe is visiting again?'

But Jack didn't answer because he'd just realised they'd left the soccer ball at the park.

THE MYSTERIOUS THIEF

'Has anyone seen my sunglasses?' asked
Mum as she picked up her keys, ready to
walk out the door.

Jack and Dad burst out laughing.

'They're on your head!' crowed Jack,
collapsing onto the sofa.

'You think you're so funny,' sniffed
Mum, whipping the glasses into her bag,
'but you weren't laughing when you lost
your skateboard last week.'

'That's right, Jack,' said Dad. 'You were about to ring the police, remember, when I found it under your bed.'

'Yeah well, you didn't find it on my *head*, did you?'

Mum giggled. 'Now that would have looked funny.'

'I know a story about mysterious disappearances,' Jack said slowly.

'Oh, do you now!' said Dad. 'Well, I'm ready for a mystery. Pity you have to go out, darling.' Dad winked at Jack.

'A Tashi mystery?' asked Mum, flinging her bag down on the table. 'Why should *I* miss out? Just because *I'm* the woman here, I have to go out and do the shopping.' Mum glared at Dad. 'Well, I'm just not having it!'

'No, neither am I,' agreed Dad. 'It's plainly unfair. Think how many women in history have missed out on fabulous stories–'

'Fascinating conversations–'

'Really good jokes–'

'Just because they had to go out shopping,' finished Dad. 'So, sweetheart, why don't you sit down here beside me and we'll change the course of history right now.'

'Deal,' said Mum.

'So,' began Jack, 'the whole thing started with Ah Chu.'

'Oh dear,' said Mum reaching for the tissues, 'are you getting a cold?'

'No,' sighed Jack. 'Remember Ah Chu, Tashi's friend back in the old country?'

'Ah yes, Ah Chu,' grinned Dad.

'Well, things had been mysteriously disappearing in the village. One morning Ah Chu stumped up the path to Tashi's house and spluttered, "You'll never believe what was taken from our place last night – my old *undies*! They were hanging on the washing line!"

'Ooh, yuk,' said Dad. 'Who'd want to steal second-hand undies?'

'Exactly,' said Jack. 'Then Lotus Blossom ran up close behind and said, "Guess what – the thief came to Precious Aunt's house last night and took her painted silk fan!"

'They were all quiet for a moment, thinking. "We'll have to put a stop to this," Tashi said at last. "Two visits in one night and there's no pattern to what is taken. It's always a mixture of valuable and useless things, like your broken spinning top last week, Lotus Blossom. People have started buying locks for their doors; we've never had to do that before."

'"I think it could be someone like the Foo brothers – they'd do it for a dare," said Lotus Blossom.

'"Maybe, but I don't think those boys would take things that people treasured. Like your grandfather's gold watch," Tashi argued.

'"I don't know," said Ah Chu. "Some of their friends would dive in first and think later."

'"All right," said Tashi, "for the next few days we'll play with them after school. There would have to be a great pile of things in their room by now, too much to hide easily."

'Four days later, the three friends met again. "Well, that was a waste of time," said Lotus Blossom crossly.

'"It was your idea," Ah Chu reminded her. "And I don't know what Ping's mother thought when she came in and found you looking through her cupboards. Just as well Tashi was able to think of a good excuse."

'"Anyway," Lotus Blossom went on as though Ah Chu hadn't spoken, "I think we have overlooked the obvious person."

'"Who?"

'"Your Uncle Tiki Pu. He's the most
dishonest person in the village."

'Ah Chu looked uncomfortable but
Tashi didn't mind. It was true. "But why
would he take underwear and broken
toys?"

'"To put us off the scent!" Lotus
Blossom cried triumphantly.

'Tashi wasn't sure, but he agreed to go
to Tiki Pu's house that afternoon because
he knew his uncle was out playing cards
with some visiting merchants. After an
hour's rummaging through the mess that
Tiki Pu lived in, they did not find one
thing that had been stolen.

'"Now I suppose we'll have to put all this jumble back," groaned Ah Chu.

'"I don't see why," said Lotus Blossom. "He'll never notice the difference." As she spoke she turned towards the door. Standing there was Tiki Pu.

'"Looking for something?" he asked in a nasty, silky voice.

'There was a long silence. Tashi swallowed. "I came to ask you to dinner tonight, Uncle, and we were just tidying your room for you while we waited."

'Tiki Pu didn't believe a word of it, but he gave Tashi a false smile and said, "Tell your mother I'd be delighted to come and that she mustn't go to too much trouble."

'"That means he'll expect all his favourite dishes," groaned Tashi as they walked home. "My mother will kill me."

'A few minutes later Tashi was running up his garden path. He popped his head in the kitchen window and called, "Tiki Pu said he'd love to come to dinner tonight, Mum, and you mustn't go to too much trouble."

'"What? Why–" She dropped her pan.

'"I'll be back soon," said Tashi quickly, as he ran after the others.

'They walked on in silence until Ah Chu said suddenly, "A funny thing happened last night. I woke up just before first light and felt a bit empty. So I went to the kitchen to look for a little snack. I was just eating a bowl of cold noodles at the window when I saw your grandmother go past. She was walking along as if it was bright daylight, not hesitating, although she didn't have a lantern and it was black night."

'"Where did she go?"

'"I don't know. The darkness swallowed her up as soon as she left the light from the window."

'"The path from your house only leads to the forest," said Lotus Blossom quietly.

'Tashi felt a shiver of fear. "We'll take turns to keep watch," he said quickly. "I'll start tonight."

'Tashi's eyes grew heavy during the long night and every now and again he had to creep about the house to stay awake. Even so, his head was nodding when the sound of a door clicking shut jerked him to his feet.

'His grandmother was already moving down the path towards the village. Tashi followed, his heart like lead as his beloved grandma stopped at Hai Ping's house. She came out a moment later carrying a copper kettle and walked briskly on, past Ah Chu's door and into the forest.

'Just as Ah Chu had said, she didn't seem to need a lantern and Tashi almost had to walk on her heels so he would not lose her in the dark.

'And so, when she stopped suddenly at a small cave opening in the mountainside, Tashi ran into her back.

'"Tashi! What are *you* doing here?" She looked about her. "And what am *I* doing here?"

'"You were sleepwalking, Grandma,"
Tashi told her gently, and took the copper
kettle from her hand. "And I'm afraid it is
you who has been taking all the things
from the village."

'Together they pushed aside the bushes
in front of the cave and by the light of the
rising moon they could see all the missing
things.

'"There's Mrs Wang's carpet," cried
Grandma in horror.

'"And Not Yet's hammer."

'"And Luk Ahead's ebony ruler,"
moaned Grandma.

'"AND MY RED POTTED ORCHID!"
bellowed a great voice behind them.

'They spun around and there was the
wicked Baron filling the opening of the
cave.

'"Grandmother didn't know she was
taking things, Baron," Tashi cried
desperately. "She's been sleepwalking. We
were just about to take them back to the
village."

'"Of course you were," scoffed the
Baron, "and I'm a tiger with purple
stripes! Well, now you've been caught."

'Grandmother began to plead with him, but Tashi cut her short. "Don't bother with him, Grandma, just pile everything onto this bed cover–"

'"Third Aunt's beautiful quilted bed cover!" wailed Grandma.

'"Never mind, Grandma, now fold the two corners like me and we can carry it all back with us tonight."

'Out of the corner of his eye, Tashi saw the Baron stoop to pick up a golden cup and slip it into his pocket.

'He said nothing, but tied the quilt corners together and turned to the Baron. "The village will know we aren't thieves when they see how we have brought everything back."

'"Not if I get back first and tell them you're only returning their goods because I caught you red-handed!"

'"Then we will just have to make sure that you don't get back first," Tashi said evenly.

'Grandmother touched the Baron's sleeve. "Please, Baron, you must know I didn't mean any harm. I couldn't help it.'

'As the Baron turned to flick off her hand, Tashi poured a cupful of sand and pebbles into his boot (using Hai Ping's good copper kettle!).

'The Baron strode ahead, but soon he slowed up, limping a little, then stopped and loosened his boot.

'"Are you having trouble, Baron?" Tashi ran up and poured some more sand and pebbles into the other boot while the Baron was emptying the first.

'"Not as much trouble as you are going to have," the Baron gloated.

'They set off again, but soon the Baron had to stop and see to his other boot. Again Tashi ran up with his kettle. The Baron was so busy cursing "these stupid stones" and "this despicable dirt" and "that lazy dolt of a shoemaker, Not Yet, who couldn't make a decent boot to save his life" that he didn't see what was going on right behind him.

'This all happened several times, with the Baron never getting very far ahead, until at last he realised what was happening.

'"You can't stop me, Tashi. I'm going to wake the village and tell them what you have been up to. Your family will be run out of town and at last I will be free of your meddling."

'The sky was beginning to lighten and down below in the village Tashi could see people stirring. The Baron was hurrying along the path. He would soon be reaching the village, raising the alarm, shouting from the square that Tashi and his family were thieves. No one would want to live beside a family who stole. They would have to leave the village that had been the family home for a hundred years.

'"Where will we go?" Grandma cried as she sank to the ground in despair.

'Tashi had just one last trick to try. He put his fingers to his lips and gave a piercing whistle.

'He didn't have long to wait. Very quickly there was a crashing through the trees and out leapt his dog, Pongo.

'"Come, Pongo," Tashi called as he ran after the Baron. The Baron looked over his shoulder when he heard them coming and smiled scornfully.

'"Guard him!" Tashi ordered. "Pongo, stay!"

'The Baron sneered. "That animal was my creature, you don't think he will obey *you* now, do you?" He glared down at Pongo. "SIT!"

'"Guard!" Tashi repeated desperately.

'Pongo looked from one to the other. He hesitated, his pink tongue lolling.

'"*SIT*, YOU IDIOT DOG!" the Baron shouted.

'Pongo made up his mind. He bounded
over to the Baron and barked. He circled
him, snarling, until the Baron dropped to
his knees.

'"Good boy, Pongo," Tashi beamed.
"Guard!"

'Tashi ran back to Grandmother. "Come
on, Grandma. We're nearly there."

'It was amazing how quickly Grandma
revived once she saw the Baron cowering
before Pongo the Brave. "Make yourself
comfortable, Baron," she crowed. "You'll
be there for some time."

'As soon as they arrived at the village square, Tashi rang the Magic Bell. When everyone had gathered around, he showed them their missing treasures and explained what had happened. People tutted and looked at each other in wonder but they were all so pleased to see their goods again, they were soon smiling and nodding to Grandma. Someone noticed how exhausted she was and brought over a chair. Another gave her a cup of tea.

'This was too much for Grandma and she had a little weep. "She'll feel much better after that," said Third Aunt, who knew about such things.

'Tashi thought it was probably time to release the Baron. So he gave three sharp whistles. In a flash Pongo came bouncing up, but the Baron wasn't far behind. He pushed importantly through the crowd.

'"Quiet everyone! I have something to tell–"

'"Good morning, Baron," Tashi stepped up beside him and smiled at the villagers. "The Baron met us coming down the mountain but his heels were so sore he told us to come on ahead." The Baron tried to push in front of Tashi and started to speak again.

'Tashi raised his voice. "I was just about to tell everyone how you helped us and how you put Wise-as-an-Owl's golden cup in your pocket so it wouldn't fall out of the quilt. Your left pocket," he added helpfully.

'"The Baron looked down at Tashi with furious eyes. Slowly he put his hand into his pocket and pulled out the golden measuring cup. He and Tashi stared at each other long and hard.

'"Just so, Tashi," he said stiffly, as he handed the cup to Wise-as-an-Owl with a little bow.

'They all had a party that night to celebrate getting their things back. And Grandma tied a string around her ankle and hooked it up to a bell on her door. But she never did sleepwalk again.'

Jack stretched and nudged his dad. 'Don't tell me *you* are asleep.'

'Huh? No, no, I was just thinking. Your Uncle Joe was a bit of a sleepwalker when he was young. Sleepwalked right into the girls' dormitory one night at school camp.'

'Yeah?' said Jack. 'So, how about we *all* go out shopping, and while we're there, we could get me an ice-cream?'

'Yep,' said Mum, standing up, 'and don't forget the organic broccoli.'

'How could we?' said Dad, and went to find his shoes.